Rhymes to Read

Jungle Home

by Ann Bryant

Illustrated by
Andy Elkerton

W
FRANKLIN WATTS
LONDON•SYDNEY

About this book

Rhymes to Read are designed for children who are ready to start reading alone. They can also be used by an adult to share with a child.

The books provide excellent support for developing phonological awareness, helping the child to recognise sounds and sound-symbol relationships. The poems are perfect to read aloud and the strong rhythms, rhymes and repetition will help build confidence and encourage reading and rereading for pleasure.

Reading tips for adults sharing the book with a child:

1. Make reading fun! Choose a time to read when you and the child are relaxed and have time to share the story.
2. Talk about the story before you start reading. Look at the cover and the blurb. What might the story be about? Why might the child like it?
3. Encourage the child to retell the story, using the pictures and rhymes to help. The puzzles at the back of the book provide a good starting point.
4. Give praise! Remember that small mistakes need not always be corrected.
5. For an extra activity you could ask the child to make up some alternative rhymes for the story or their own brand new rhyme!

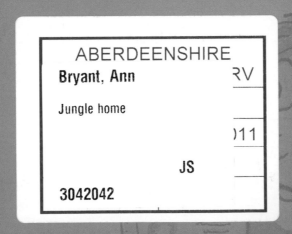

Mr Gray sits at home, very rich but all alone.

In the jungle far away,
rainbow lizards
seem to say,

"Please don't take
our home away!"

5

Mr Gray reads a book.
"A jungle dying?
I must look!"

In the jungle far away,
frogs and fruit bats
seem to say,

8

"Please don't take our home away!"

9

Mr Gray gets on a plane.

He flies through clouds
and sun and rain.

In the jungle far away,
bees and beetles
seem to say,

"Please don't take our home away!"

Mr Gray finds a river.
He sees the trees
that shake and shiver.

In the jungle just
beside him,

monkeys from the
treetops guide him.

"Can you help us, please?" they say. "Don't let them take our home away!"

"I'll buy your home," says Mr Gray. "Then you and all your friends can stay!"

Now Mr Gray sits at home,
not so rich, but not alone!

Puzzle 1

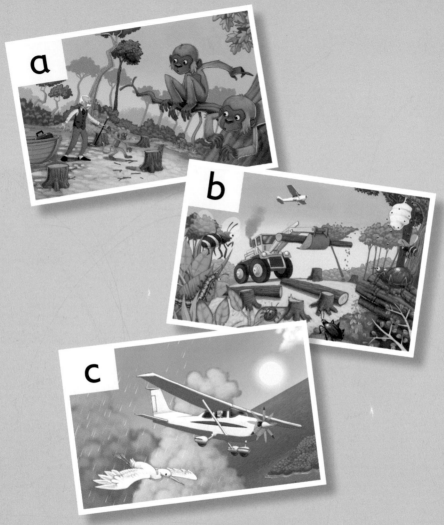

Put the pictures in the correct
order and retell the story.

river

trees

shake

shiver

away

take

say

lizard

Find the rhyming words above.

Turn over for answers!

Answers

Puzzle 1

The correct order is: c, b, a.

Puzzle 2

The rhyming words are:

a. river, shiver

b. away, say

First published in 2011 by
Franklin Watts
338 Euston Road
London
NW1 3BH

Franklin Watts Australia
Level 17/207 Kent Street
Sydney
NSW 2000

Text © Ann Bryant 2011
Illustration © Andy Elkerton 2011

The rights of Ann Bryant to be
identified as the author and Andy Elkerton
as the illustrator of this Work have been
asserted in accordance with the Copyright,
Designs and Patents Act, 1988.

A CIP catalogue record for this book is
available from the British Library.

ISBN 978 1 4451 0292 4 (hbk)
ISBN 978 1 4451 0298 6 (pbk)

Series Editor: Melanie Palmer
Series Advisor: Catherine Glavina
Series Designer: Peter Scoulding

Printed in China

Franklin Watts is a division of Hachette Children's Books,
an Hachette UK company. www.hachette.co.uk